T0354844

You're Going To Panic and That's Ok

ARMAND FISCHIONE

authorHOUSE

AuthorHouse™
1663 Liberty Drive
Bloomington, IN 47403
www.authorhouse.com
Phone: 1 (800) 839-8640

Published by AuthorHouse 05/26/2020

ISBN: 978-1-7283-5765-2 (sc)
ISBN: 978-1-7283-5764-5 (e)

Library of Congress Control Number: 2020905778

Psychiatric Evaluation

Who are you?
Are you a fish?
A nut?
Are you circumcised?
Are you uncircumcised?
Are you a rebel?
The next John Sinclair?
The next Kurt Cobain?
The savior of rock 'n' roll?
The well-to-do Christian at your school?
The badass who smokes pot and fucks all the time?
The first person to kick out the jams?
Are you bisexual?
Are you a vegan obsessed with your body?
A milf?
A skin care technician?
A poet?
A beatnik?
A phony?
A shit talker?
A shoegazer?
The Beatles?
Relavent.

FAKE DEEP

I took some cheese from the mouse trap
Now I can't get out
I took a bath in the fountain of youth
Now there is a drought
Conquistador, that's what I am
Can't overtake fear, but can overtake land

I rub the hilt of my silver blade
Across my withered tongue
Between these popcorn eyes you see
Those kernels have not sprung
At the hillside top you told me no one makes it out
All the bird baths, still the drought

Sometimes I feel elevated
Sometimes I derail
I'm fighting for my life and love
But only I can hear
I'm elevated by the thought of this all ending soon
Fountain of youth, come save me, pull me through

Love is not a two way street
Like the way you spill your wine
I love you like a serpent loves
Adam and Eve's mind
I left you frantic like a dog kicked in the eye
In the doghouse, sitting around, getting high

I do not long for sex no more
I do not like the taste
You look me in the eyes and say

That I have taken you away
Well how can that be done when all you see is thrown away?
But even still, after all this, I'll gladly take the blame

You seem a little tense my dear
Come lie down by my side
Eat my dinner little one
And do save room for pie
But please don't tell me what to do
Let me just get high

AFTER THE AFTERLIFE

A lifeless silhouette
creeping through the darkness
Aching
the sky is his never-ending

like a partner in crime
they never leave each other

I ache
and shouted to an empty room
torn apart time after time
lifeless performance art

watching the party go on
wondering what to do after the afterlife

Lost dreams of innocence
float away
lost
away

love and lust enter the room
wondering what to do after the afterlife

I sang a song
in the key of C
torn apart time after time
lifeless performance art

watching the party go one
wondering what to do after the afterlife

COSA NOSTRA

Empathy can't save me now
Neither can this feeling
It's like the world is turning black
The fishing pole is reeling
I'm never one to turn away
A friend in need is worth living
Sad to see it happen

I met myself at a movie theatre
At a double feature for one
Popcorn, drinks, candy, soda
We had a lot of fun
I asked myself how I did it
How I climbed out from this trench
He said I shouldn't look too hard
The valleys are covered in mist

I called his bluff
I slicked my hair
I'm waiting for my ride
The ramification of my reincarnation
That's for me to decide

TRUE BLUE

I'm swimming in the ocean, waiting to touch you
I'm standing in the city, waiting to feel you
In a room without a window, you were picture perfect scenery
In a black and white movie, you were technicolor beauty

Dancing in the dark, unknowing of our fate
Death is at our door, knocking half past eight
But we don't seem to mind, you and I
We're just staring into each others eyes
As if our souls are about to leave us all behind

We did everything we said
Except be there for each other
I'm swimming in the ocean, waiting to touch you
I'm standing in the city, waiting to feel you

AUTOPSIES

Hey baby, what it do(?)
Autopsies of me and you
They don't make sense, but we don't ask questions(?)
Birthday gifts were never unpleasant
The middle of the road was where I left you

SPACEY INSTRUMENTAL

Couldn't read the clock as I got up in the morning
Floating in your arms I drifted back to sleep
Finally woke up, cooking breakfast with style
Vibrations in the morning air, crisp and cool
Crashing like a tidal wave in sea green delight
The stars align over all our reservations

Prop telephone calling for my uncle
Picking strawberries off of purple vines
One dimly lit candle by the windowsill
Glitter on the angel dust
Whirlpool down the ocean floor

Spaceman, spaceman
Meet me halfway
Make my thoughts turn yellow
Turn my mind to clay
With your silly putty thoughts
Of Turkish delight served cold
Show me how to use it
Show me how to abuse it
Show me how to reminisce

COLORS

We went to prom at the very last minute
Before they closed the doors on us
We got dressed, decided to sit on it
In tardiness we trust
Mental vacations take way too long
Moral compass off the course
Spent 2 months in those trenches alone
Led me right to the source

The grass is green and my nails are dirty
I raise my fist at God
In this room it's getting hot
I'm holding on to old flaws
I'm holding you in my arms
You took me into your room
Made me see colors I had never seen before
Hopefully you can see them too

This sun in the corner of your picture
Can be drawn in without me

BEATLEMANIA

Come out of your body, baby
Don't be shy to leave, just walk out of your body
Continue our mission, with your permission
We can continue this fling
We can drive by all the trees and the lights
Watching all the road signs fade into the night
Just me and you, another Bonnie & Clyde comparison
We can roll up while it's windy

It's a problem we all face
Falling in and out of grace
Floating on, flying through space
Broken pencil, cannot trace

She's my favorite form of empathy
She's my favorite strain of bud
She's my favorite 8-track tape
She's my special kind of fun

OUTSTANDING LOVE

I have nothing to give you
I am nothing to everyone
You're an outstanding move
While I'm out standing in the rain
Let's spend the night together
I'll crawl out your back window
You were an outstanding move
My scent is on your sheets
Anxiety is kept alive

You can't shake this feeling
You can't get it off your tongue
They think about outstanding moves
Lay it down on the table
But I say keep smoking
Keep a smile while you do it
My love for you is outstanding
You're an outstanding move
I want to taste your lips
And call you mine

If I could be at home now
If I could be by your side
The grass would be greener
The moon wouldn't need the tides
The ocean would subside
Into the teardrops that I cry
To think, after all this time
Our love was outstanding

VACANT

Sleigh ride to your house
Box of chocolates, brand new blouse
Spilling wine on my white shirt
Make a scene
Pretty things come to dance
Ready for a new romance
Mezzo forte's how we fuck
Make a scene

Car show right down the hall
Dive-bomb robocall
Remains of love that's been
Better things that time has seen

Who stays for the mentally vacant?
Studies of war and love adjacent
Down that withered path we go
Looking for the moon glow
Who stays for the mentally vacant?

FAVORITE CARD TRICK

I'm here, then I'm not
I'm the belief beside your faith
Coconut oil slides on your skin
My favorite picnic, beloved card trick
She shows up in Prada
Watches and bracelets divine
Decals on her car bumper
Smoke you out like no one's ever done before

I'm here, then I'm not
I'm the belief beside your faith
And there's nothing that she will die for
Inside her head to the point of extinction

Then you go into her room
You're shaking with anticipation
Her hands cup around you
Her lips are above you
She is your new belief

LOVE

Love makes the world go round
Love makes the rivers crash
Love makes lovers lash
Love

Love is like a brand new car
Love is like the setting sun
Love is like a hot cross bun
Love

Trash-bag blues, wake up drunk
Love
Trash-bag blues, fake it 'till you make it
Love

Love is not in control, it's the heart and soul
Of the minds shining diamond that turns into coal
Love

If Judas were to say he loves you
Would you say you love him back?
Love

I doubt it, baby
I really doubt it

Love is a knife to the prick
Wounds are deep, no going back

What's your sign?
Love

PUPPETEER

If you want me to
I will dance for you
On a restaurant table
In the middle of the day
And if I break my leg
On the table
It'll be ok

If you want me to
I will change for you
Into another man
That's new
And abort myself
To make you
Happy again

If you want me to
I will drink for you
And pass out drunk
On the kitchen table
Wondering "where did you go?"

If you want me to
I will cheat for you
And make you cry
And die inside
While I'm away
Having fun

If you want me to
I will bleed for you
And slit my wrists at noon
So you can see me soon
Instead of never

If you want me to
In spite of you
I could move to the zoo
And live with the lions
And the bears
And never notice the difference

CACTUS

There's a storm coming, and you just jump in the puddles
The hurricane looks like a miniature horse on wheels
You look pale, comatose; a death row meal
If you didn't smile in that moment, I would have left you for dead

You're starting to look and act like my father
I need some medicine, get me medicine from my father
You look pale, comatose; a death row meal
If you didn't smile in that moment, I would have left you for dead

These moments with you
Make me feel like I'm living
But it's the way you left me for dead

MY BEAUTIFUL, MY LOVE

You make my dreams reality
My beautiful, my love
I don't feel alone anymore
My beautiful, my love
You're 10 violins playing in unison
Fuck the orchestra, I want to hear you

I'll never let go
My beautiful, my love
I pace around the room
My beautiful, my love
I want to hear your tuba's playing, my love
Where's the orchestra, I want to hear you

I want to go out like James Dean
I want you there with me
My beautiful, my love
Tell your friends what we did together
My beautiful, my love
When I look at you, I see thunder in your eyes
My beautiful, my love
I wander into your room, see you with somebody new
Suddenly, I'm a murderer
I'll kill whoever comes between us
Until his breath is gone

My beautiful, my love
Never cross my path again
I'll walk the other way
I'll drag your name in the mud
To your new lover, your lover's lover

To God and the devil
Until I get my way

"How evil this has gotten"
My beautiful, my love
Just close your eyes
Wake up from this fever dream

OLD AGE

You sit at home
Decomposed, all alone
Walk to the shower
Bake a cake
Bare faced, Sharron Tate
Walk to the shower

At the gala there stood harps
Made of sex wax & angel bark
Walk to the shower
Bloody shoe prints on the stairs
Cross the line, skin the bride
Walk to the shower

"This could take a thousand years"
Our car rides ripen with silence
Try, but you can no longer hide it
Walk to the shower
Lock the front door, lamb to the slaughter
Moon's out full, isn't that a miracle
Cling to the daytime, cry when it's dark
Praying to God, you haven't lost your spark
So run to the hills, set camp for the night
So run to the hills, see how brightly you burn out

My love, my beauty, she exists for pleasure
Just try to come between us, our love won't tether
Tastefully, yet serene
Walk to the shower
You and me, we're in this for life
Visions of you, matrimony, my wife
Tastefully

GREENERI

Left the water running in your shower
Hope you don't mind, I had to go
((Fuck your honesty, your privacy, your faith))
((Stick it up your ass))
The commute should take 10 minutes without traffic
((Why do I care about you?))
((All you do is make me sad))
But by God, dead or alive, I want to make a family for us
No matter the cost, my freedom
All for my baby, my love
((I can't believe you came back))
((Even after the fact))
You might think you know me now, but by the end of this, you will
((Find me. You never will))
((Guys like you can't walk straight))
Trust me, baby, trust me

How do you start off your day?
You might run, you might bike, tread water for a few
Walk down the street just to see what's new
He's got his daddy's fear in his eyes
Look at him squirm
Go ahead, tell them it's for a different reason
He was never around for you
Refused to take you to the zoo
Cheated out of every opportunity to be with you
Now that you're off and gone what can he do?
Make out empty promises while you stand there in the rain?
No!
Fuck that!
Get angry!

Kill!
Anarchy!
He never believed in you
Why should you? Ugh, go to school
It's a sad, sad, sad song
But I know I'll get back on track
Tomorrow is a new day, I'm climbing up the rafters
For the sake of my song, my life, my pursuit of happiness

So don't be nervous
When God's greater purpose
Isn't there to catch you fall
Turn away from the pain you revived so much later on
Turn away, turn this page, turn your back on me
This is when the sun sets in the Arizona rain

YOU

You slid right between my fingers
for me and me alone

DEFINITELY, ABSOLUTELY

Screaming to the wall I face
The earth falls without a trace
My insides are interlaced
Punk rock, blunt to the face
Everlasting covenant, this body of mine
Rolling in the dunes
It's crazy how life works
Take my secret to the grave
Other people taking my secrets to the grave
Take you to my place

You're alone, and you say you like that feeling
I'm with my friends, and I get that lonely feeling
Claustrophobic clusterfuck
A day in the life
Gets me so fucking down
My pride is in a dimly lit room
Where piranhas and tiny fish swim
To the top
Just to breathe
But they can't
So they proceed
To kill themselves
Head above the freezing cold water
Decomposing, I suppose
Mother and Father be kind to those who drown

I know your location
I know this deep water you swim under
Madness in the pond
Green scum

DIVE

Here she stands, with my heart in her hand
Bike chain renegade on the edge of my holster
Churches full of liars, sinners, and saints
She's a God amongst men, you will quake
She's sitting at home not even thinking about me

You told me to watch my back
That's no fun, I can't see my face
Hit me with the force of 10
Give me that triple double you always talk about
I'm a waste of space, that's why we don't talk, right?
Friends don't talk to me like they used to
Starting to think I'm toxic
Maybe I'm not the crazy one
Maybe it's the crazy talking
But I'm not crazy

That line was garbage
My lines are garbage
I can do better

I'm better than everyone
I don't need to be told that
I hate phonies
I feel like the biggest one
I'm better than you
I don't know what's going on
You think I need Jesus
Call me a cab, take me to church
You're coming with me, get the hearse
I just want to be home

Let me go home
My mood swings are starting

I wanted to get higher with you than with anyone
I wanted you to be terrible
I wanted to lose you

BACKGROUND MUSIC

Grabbing my innocence with my own two hands
Doo-wop playing while you give me head
Lamp shade princess with caviar eyes
Cocaine dream-line heading straight for disaster
Foam from your cup overflowing like a waterfall
Lick the sides, I just bought that dresser
When you were little you lived in a greenhouse
Martians and spaceships were the only way out

Detective knocking on your door
English lad about 6'4
Said he heard footsteps around the house
Nothing was heard, not even a mouse
And my mistress is away, business trip in Cabo
Fake hugs and face masks are the games we play

My name is easy but my face is distorted
Don't watch my shoulders, they won't sway
Pretty bird flying out, so common
Fly away from me
Don't know when I'll see it again
Don't know if I really care
I hate parties, they make me uneasy

But I've seen the tapes, studied them alone
Convertible, orange interior with the bloodshot eyes
Speed freak posers with nothing to lose
Ship captain blues with holes in his boat
We know what you are
Background music for the boys

DON'T SAY ANYTHING

Blue sympathy from a telephone wire
Hanging tree says guns for hire

Superfly in a venus trap
Listening to Blood on the Tracks

Kiss your thighs, make me blue
King of necks, I always bruise

Can't keep a secret for too long now
Depression, roped in like cattle

Don't say anything if you don't mean it
Don't say anything if you cannot speak it

BABY WANTS IT ALL

Looking good in that white dress
She flaunts me
((Now we're getting somewhere))
Blue dream is what you wanted me to call you
Adderall crushed on the countertop
Cooking something up while I'm away
We don't talk anymore

Lotion in the nighttime
Day cream for my may queen
Blue dream in the bowl
Take a pill to get low
Acting up, oh well, whatever
Kiss you on the open mouth
Mushrooms in the midsummer
Take my hand and take the plunge

My love for her is like a fridge
Keep it cool, but leave some room
Her family doesn't like me, but why should I care
I'm being myself, there's nothing wrong with that
She's doing her, and we're going places
Me & her
Taking the plunge

Baby wants it all
The credit cards and white lines
Baby wants it all
From bloody sheets and dirty streets
She's come into her own

TURTLES

Cloudy perception, foggy brain
Velvet hands with scent of vinegar
Watch face, 3 clocks, body of Christ
Blue lagoon, milky way, forced perspective
Cartoons & movies with the curtains drawn
Tennis court star, Nikes on foot
Shit, I fucked up

Wanted to be Hendrix until I tried 'cid
Statue of David, star-spangled harlot
Frozen dinners with the father of my bride
My mother's in Europe with some guy I've never met
It's been a year and I still can't roll 'woods
((The bowl still crackles, though))
No one I know is worthy of me
Try as they may, no ones on my level
I saw him and I saw the end of the road
I'm afraid of going psycho
I see the cul-de-sac and now I'm fine
((Did you know I didn't know the meaning of cul-de-sac until I was 7?))
Filming your girlfriend just for the hell of it
It was your idea for an open relationship
Everybody knows I'm a piece of shit
Sleazy, no good, might fuck your wife
Holding out my hands reaching for a sign
Pissing in a bucket just to keep it mellow
Know who you trust, know who you're with
Trust runs out like a parking meter
Suicide runs on the field
Suicide runs in my head

This is my blood, drink it and live
Dior button-up just to keep it clean
Adolescence was something that never existed
Polo pullover bumping Kid Cudi
Mr. Rager, Mojo So Dope, All Along
Lobster meal with my baby in that red dress
Suicide runs in the family
Suicide runs in my head

Mary Jane, Marijuana, LSD, and me
In the parking lot behind the Double Tree
1993, Kurt Cobain & me
Parking garage can only hold 2
Asylum seekers, digging tunnels
Malibu & orange juice, Miami summers
Rodeo, track 10, for the time being
Never a car guy, too busy collecting my thoughts
Thumbs up, slam the door in my face
Fuck social media, I'm going viral off these tabs
Nose bloody like an all night bender
Tooth fairy, wet dreams, psilocybin nightmare
End it off like this: I miss you

NIKE SB

Hair long, down to my shoulders
Brad Pitt, Johnny Depp, River Phoenix
Dunks double-knotted as I'm biking through the streets
Diving board sparkles like seltzer
Hell is hot like a sauna
Detroit Partnership, kill the Kennedys
Beat it up, sweating like a sauna
By 21, I'll be a memory
I don't know why, I just expect it
Jolly Green Giants stomping ground
Jesus Christ, I'm stepping down
Dead-shot, right in her eye
Kiss my baby on the lips
Treat it nice, slide on the wood
Biting baby's neck, it's understood
Pussy Neapolitan, put the cherry on top
Baby's double crossed, doesn't know what she wants
Jim Jones with the persuasion
Charles Manson with the acid
Darth Maul with the saber
I'm a lover not a fighter
There's love in war
Buddies of mine who show up bar'd out
Bar none, by far, they can't function tonight

But now it's cold outside and I miss you

Gibson loud like a house alarm
Bong hitting harder than it should
Picture this moment forever
Wouldn't know you if I could

Custom chain made just for me
Confidence is coming back
Feel like I put you on the map
Baby needs to throw it back
Then I give it back to you
Pussy in a body bag
Redhead, Hermione
That's when it happened

7 years old drawing lamps and harpoons
9 years old watching cartoons
Born wealthy, bought the word money
Boat parties, Yacht parties, bargains, funny money
Money up front
Baby girl, American
Frank Ocean on the dashboard
Baby's hand in my lap
First class to Michigan
No big deal, no big shakes
Get laid on the sofa
No one has to know

TARANTULA

Noir lighting over the furnished table
Kiss me like you mean it
The night you put my hand under your skirt was insane
Scratches on your back like stripes on a zebra
Scratches on my bed post
With that, I'll never call you again

I know we're not in love, but could you just hold me?
Soprano when I'm in those guts
No one understood who I was when I was little
Guitar strumming every night and day

Ladder going straight to heaven
Jesus waiting to give me a necklace
Biking just to clear my head
11's on my feet
AJ doesn't know, he was just mislead
Reciting the rosary in the garden that night
Nirvana is approaching
Nirvana is in the air
Nirvana is spiteful
Nirvana is forgiving
Nirvana is sobriety
Nirvana is you

Candy flipped baby, strawberry shortcake
Talk about this later on
Eyes in the skull, mouth in an O
Teeth on the neck, fingers in the mouth
How obscene, take me to the judge

Treat me like Ginsberg, knick away my pride
One by one, until I collapse on the floor
2 tabs, tongue makes a blanket
Kiss me right now or this never happened

SON'S & DAUGHTER'S

So the night turns to day
Light is no longer on your side
Eros is watching keenly upon your withered foreplay
The running gun blues burning through your high

Presented with the statistics of abuse
The darkness of the night forms like a web
Stretching out past the trees like a noose
They said it before, you're better off dead

You say it's just a drill
Your intellect will get the best of you
As your son and daughter's take the pills
Your son and daughter's bid adieu

And though you miss the goodnight kisses
Your linen stinks of silent death
You stoop so low on your hits and misses
You couldn't stand to hear your last breath

You had preparations upon preparations
Desires that had to be had
Books to fill, pages to write
You didn't once think it's a sin

You have your mistress and your letters
You had her love and total trust
My savior on a shoestring
Demands that I don't trust

You had anticipations upon anticipations
Crucifixes hung upon your wall
You portray a bigger mans fixations
In a world that's oh-so small

So take your pills
You won't be seeing those anymore
As your son and daughter's take the pills
Your son and daughter's bid adieu

INDIGO

Space is such a cliche place
Why can't we ever go to Mars
Why do we have to sweep the room
While the rover does our job
Imagine me, flying away on a rocket ship
The grass is greener on the moon
I'd like to visit it

Space is such a scary place
It's lonely in the abyss
I'd like to bring a stack of books
And an airbag, in case I get sick
I'd keep a rover as a pet
Call him Sparky, Stitch, or Gizmo
We would look up at the stars above
And see our darkness made of indigo

Space is just so ordinary
I'm starting to feel bored
Auto pilot talks to himself
And my mother's overboard
Distress calls to my father
But nothing will come through
Space is such a dangerous place
It's not fit for me or you

In the year 3004
They will find my shattered bones
They'll use me up for science
My rover will go home

HOLISTIC

This is my death, time wrote it down before
God laughs at your fate, then closes the doors
Milky way dreaming down a moonbeam stream
Cranium canal, dying for attention

When you're born, you are the setting sun
When laid to rest, you're paid to run
Talk to the woman you love so dearly
Cranium carnage, dying for vitality

Car breaks down on the side of the road
No signal, no stress, nowhere to call home
Sunlight is beaming on you
Vultures fly around in circles
And yet here you stand complete

Self-diagnosing yourself to sleep
Ferris wheel rides and a big stuffed bear
Decapitation of the head honcho
Blow dry the dry blood on the kitchen sink
Self-diagnosing yourself to sleep
Past does not define you
More than the sum of your broken parts
Lactate the pain from swollen breasts of creativity
Join in the fun, hit and run
Drown yourself to sleep

Smoke a little, green out
Hold my hand, pass out

BLACK SABBATH

Venice sunrise, orange of my eye
Mustache masquerade, music box serenade
Stripper, you should she the way she moves
Now she walks among the hermit crabs and fights for time

God is dead
We touched priests before they could touch us
Isn't that just like us?
L.A. is full of rainbows
We killed him

You look just like Elton John
In a Dodgers suit
Oversized and pretty
You're my only special baby

And for a minute there, I thought we were real
Being together was too good to be true
You knew the nooks and crannies of my mind
Now you're just another dead memory

Sail on you alcoholic
Down a 5th and then a shot
Swerving off the 17
Your head becomes your liver

COFFEE

Once I knew a girl named Claire
With a voice like thorns and flowers in her hair
We talked among our coffee and time
And soon enough our time was bare

Once I knew a girl named Laney
With a voice like a lady and eyes like a baby
We talked among our coffee and time
She looked at me like I was crazy

Once I knew a boy named Chance
With fire in his eyes and with a passing glance
Said "look me in the eyes, be careful what you find"
But he closed them before I could

I soon walked into a cave
Where the people are down and none have shaved
And when they try to run away
They get closer and closer to their grave

The days went by, they turned to years
I stayed in a little shack with a room
No one could hear me dry my tears

Most of those who think they can help
End up making their lives a living hell
Talking among their coffee and time
But put both of them back on the shelf

For 40 days I woke up shaking
My arms and legs went numb
God was weeping that day
He saw what I've become

I slashed, and carved, and cut
Everyday I would sit and conduct
Talking among our razors and wine
I stood along that thin white line

I've spat in the eyes of fools
Of those, by thought, were worthless tools
I walked out and was wished the best
But the path we walk is not always what we choose

Once I laid with girls in twos
Took a thousand men to see if it was true
My passion was known across the land
But only known by few

I got better, and I was free
I was a Cadillac, faster than a bee
Was I the fastest of them all?
Not fast enough, I see

I wrote a letter to my brother
Who I've heard is seeing another
Talking among our coffee and time
He looked right at me and shuddered

I drink my coffee sip by sip
Until one little drop sits
I sat down and began to laugh
And made another cup

12:35 AM

I knew a women
Who came by every winter
And slept with me
On a fold out mattress

I knew a girl
With a laugh as big as Asia
And amphetamine dreams
Who came to say goodbye

I knew a mother
Who said goodbye to everything
Even the oranges, and the pears
To the tissues and the columns on the wall

LOVERS REVENGE

The door to my bedroom creaks open slightly
These are the stories that degrade and abuse
Digging tunnels, planting seeds of truth
Baby has nowhere to go but to mama
Flashing lights are what I look forward to
Bird eggs by my doorstep waiting to be returned
Their souls vacate, lost in the wind
I get off on your fashion
Lovers Revenge

The tale of eye for an eye
Scented candles by the vitreous gel
He won't hurt you

I fought off four bears
I climbed the tallest peaks
And the sun still looks down upon me
Ambiance was something to be desired on these trips
And I'm in love with the way you plot and scheme
And I can't let you know how I want it to be
I want to notice the groceries every week or so
Do you think this is ecstasy? Maybe even bliss?
Keep laughing babe, blow me a kiss
Save it for the months that will pass us by

INVISIBLE DEFEAT

I woke up in the morning
With a pulsate-pounding headache
And as I went downstairs
I saw the young day break
The windows open slightly
And the birds they gently tweet
And suddenly I'm alone now
In this invisible defeat

I loved you like a virgin
A piece of meat to rot
You loved me like a version
Of a boy scout with his knot
You made me cut you off the rack
And the love we made was sweet
But how in the world could you expect
My invisible defeat

Don't ask me why I did it
Don't ask me if I care
We can talk about this all
'Till we shed off all our hair
With your kinky little poses
Your sex and cheap receipts
You knew me even better
In my invisible defeat

My heart, it seems, is always right
My hands are forward palms
We can drive, and drive, and drive
But can't get any farther ·

In the car, you look surprising
With your hair behind the seat
You must have been a treasure queen
In your invisible defeat

The days we spent together
I cannot exactly recall
I remember there was shouting
The rest was all a fog
Until you came with my things
You said "you've accomplished quite a feat"
I said to you "no, my love,
It's my invisible defeat"

The streets at night, they get quite lonely
Everything looks obsolete
A band inside is playing jazz
With a swinging backbeat
But I was not fixated
On the trumpet or the beat
I was only focused on the line
Of my invisible defeat

I loved you like a virgin
A piece of meat to rot
You loved me like a version
Of a boy scout with his knot
You made me cut you off the rack
And the love we made was sweet
But how in the world could you expect
My invisible defeat

SOLILOQUY

Walk with me around the boardwalk
I'm sure I'll show you off
I don't want to blow this chance
I won't persuade you otherwise
I promise I won't crap out
Inhale your scent thru those elevator doors
Passion folding like a chair
Hold my hand as you get in my car
Let's drive around town together
Cudi's on the radio
I know you love his songs
Get some rocks and you snort it
Got some buddies that'll call it
Like they say, it's darkest before dawn
Money rolling right in
You won't need me anymore
Feeling blue and lonely
Just hear me out—
Shopping sprees whenever you like
Cocaine, powder, China White
Lou Reed complex, oh my God
Don't listen to me right now
Don't talk to me right now
Don't start with that tone
You know how much that hurts
I loved you better yesterday
Shitty for me to say
I know I can do better
Feels like I can't reach you
I loved you better yesterday
I'm sure I'll show you off

Tribal gathering of the strangest folk
Green tea and smoking dope
I'm not crazy, that guy is
I'm not crazy, the sky is

Rewind
Fresh start
New day is dawning
Fading into past lives
Faded by this half-life
Scary how the world keeps turning
Even on your darkest days in life

I don't want to keep fighting like this
Can't keep hearing how my head's too thick
I love you
Kurt Cobain never had this problem
Come sit, get some dick, you'll feel better in the morning
We'll fuck again after work
Friends say you're no good for me
I think they're probably right
I ain't leaving, this is my house
What gives you the right
I'm not crazy, that guy is
I'm not crazy, the sky is

Crazy, crazy, crazy, crazy
You're the one I found here
What's a needle in a haystack
To a napkin for dry tears
Step into the light
This is crazy, isn't it?

So how are you?
So how's life?
You remarried? Guess that's life

I'm smoking good, not keeping track
Tripping good, couple tabs
Have my family, that's a fact
Have my music, thank God for that
Reading books, making movies
Distract from this insecurity
I feel every day
Ain't it funny
My mind is good, better than yours
I'm eating out, looking good
Look at you, you're floored
Remember locking me outside your door
Remember saying to myself
"I'm not crying anymore"
You thought you had me beaten
But I'm just getting started
Catch me in another life, I'll be tending to my garden

FREE FALLING IN THE BLACK HOLE

Every time I see you
Every time I die
Look both ways, cross the street
Still I see your eyes

Lindsay, I waited on you
I checked into that hotel
Checked into my own suite life
Came crashing to the ground

You don't care, I'm free falling in the black hole

LEADER'S EAT THEIR OWN

Here we are
Buried 6 feet amongst the dead
The foundations of love crumbled
And I want to die
No sign of life on the horizon
No sailors anchoring their boats

Almost everyday
Leaders eat their own
Almost everyday
The blade runs on my skin
In my lucid nightmares
A soprano
Sings throughout the night

LOTUS

When I was of the earth, I was calm and ready
My life was worth living for, my pulse was steady
Now I am an orphanage, for a soul that's past
Now my body is crumbling at a pace so fast

When I was a boy, I was happy
So full of life, so full of spunk
But now I am writing on such short notice
I used to be a flower, my name was lotus

Now I am grey, a past memory of those who lost the game
A reminder of those who have lost what they've gained
A signal to those who will lose once again
A beacon of hope to the people who choose
When to quit or when to lose

WARM SUMMER'S EVENING

Walking down a beaten path
The same one I saw not long ago
But that path is gone now
This one's full of falling snow
The breeze is cool, calm, and neat
I can feel the ground below my feet
I don't know why, but I'll try to fly
Fly away and see the light

MAN IS EVIL

Let's go to a movie
I'll get the candy
Let's invite some friends
Fake friends, one's we can't trust
Let's castrate the rapists
Mike Pence can join in too
Piss stains on the deck of the cruise
You know I love you too

Man is walking, man is evolving
Man is horny, man is thriving
Cut off his nose when he's awake
While he's driving cut his brakes
As he skids off the 101
He thinks of his past
He thinks about his lover
He thinks no one ever took him to task
No one can have what he has

Man is evil, see him kill
Public hanging is at noon
Man is evil, love is shrill
Knight him just to kill him soon

BALL & CHAIN

I played the trombone, I have danced with the devil
Weirdly composed, juxtaposition
Running into you does not feel real
I should have been gone
Made out like a bandit
Black and blue outlines like a shaving foam Santa
Cross country, back and forth, savoring banter

I walked the line between whittling and slashing
Bloodshot eyes, fucked up hairdo
Tokyo lights, I'll never get to see them
The most I can do is smile
The most I can do is be your friend
The least I can do is thank you
Blood flows down to the deepest, darkest depths

So how the fuck did this happen
When did you learn how to kill and maim
When the limelight becomes a darker shade of green
When the woman of your dreams resents your very sense of self
You sit on your thumb until it turns numb and then slowly but surely
Twist the knife one more time

I ran across the shoreline, tried to reach a payphone
But those don't exist anymore
Take your brain, put it near your heart
Ask God to make you sharp
Make it hurt
Dance with me, play the trombone

Fuck the code, fuck what you stand for
Pull whats inside you out of you for good
Like a harvester of sorrow
Let me loose, run me over

Play the trombone, dance with the devil

THE STOOGES

I now realize
Santa Fe has a price
Ignorant to think
Flowers bloom in the garden
Outside my window

You don't know me, so don't try to act like it
The razor never quits on me
Even when I want it to
But throughout this shit-faced facade
You still stand next to me

There's a song
It's been stuck in my head
For the past few weeks it's been there
Maybe it's in my head
In my mind, you're a California garage band

I miss my home and I miss my friends
I miss my car while you hold my hand
And when this shit-faced facade comes out
Don't let this shit-faced facade come out

I'm back in this mess I've made for myself
Between fucked up and fuck up
I don't know where I stand in this
I can see my own face
But I don't want to acknowledge
That this is the face of someone who's won

BEARDED LADY

When I was a boy, I was told silence made the world go 'round
Alarming as it sounds, that always stuck with me
Surprising as it, I'm running away with glee
My intuition turns to inhibition that I try to drown
I wish life could feel like glitter
I wish life wouldn't kick me down

This place I knew, is dead and gone
I know it's home, but it's dead and gone
Future and the practice of it, wish that I could see it
But like glitter, everything sparkles when in its place
Like the bearded lady, laughing at the human race
((I wish life wasn't so scary to me))

My bedpost frames are chipped of wood
My lack of defeat, enraging
I wish I could go back in time
To let you know I made it

SNOWFLAKES

To put it lightly, I broke you
It's time for me to step up to the plate
First time in a long time
I accept that I was wrong
I could have done better by you

Do snowflakes cry
When they're on the tongues
Of mother nature?
Of father earth?
Of rock formations tall and grand?
Fracking away at my love for you

TRAVERTINE BICYCLE

If I have to tell you again
Like I told you before
Mr. Macho wants out
It won't rain anymore
I saw you with another
On my travertine bicycle
You keep kneeling and hiding
From your squealing and crying

Now hold on a minute
How can you be so sure
That the cleanliness you wait for
Could be what you want
You haven't even tried to keep the peace
You haven't even wanted to be near me
You haven't told me it rains outside
You haven't told me you were the father of my bride

"Let's ride into the sunset
On your travertine bicycle
It'll be swift and easy"
It wasn't even an afterthought
Until things got grizzly

So Long

When my son is old enough
He will bear my wooden cross
When my son is old enough
He'll abuse all of our trust

ABOUT THE AUTHOR

Armand Fischione has a passion for making words as an art form. Influenced by wordsmiths such as Eminem, Tom Petty, and Kurt Cobain, Armand Fischione creates his own lane in poetry defined by his own rules.

Printed in the United States
by Book masters

Printed in the United States
By Bookmasters